"Exciting, charming, and ridiculous."
—*The Guardian*

"Incredibly funny and imaginative."
—*Sunday Express*

"I loved all the ghosties' beautifully sketched
characteristics, and the sensitive way in which King's
story helps children understand fear."
—*Daily Telegraph*

"King is very good at making children think about
their world . . . hugely inventive and charmingly
funny; early readers will adore having this book read
to them and will love trying it themselves."
—*Literary Review*

"Full of fun humor and ridiculous behavior."
—*My Child*

"Writer and illustrator have produced a
hilarious fun-packed riot."
—*Herald*

Frightfully
Friendly Ghosties

FRIGHTFULLY FRIENDLY GHOSTIES

Quercus

Nestlé Gold Award Winner

DAREN KING

Quercus

New York / London

Text © 2013 by Daren King

Illustrations © 2013 David Roberts

ISBN 978-1-62365-026-1

Distributed in the United States and Canada
by Random House Publisher Services

c/o Random House, 1745 Broadway

New York, NY 10019

For information about custom editions,
special sales, and premium and corporate purchases,
please contact the Quercus sales director
at eric.price@quercus.com.

Manufactured in the United States of America

www.quercus.com

For Rebecca

Also By Daren King

Mouse Noses on Toast
Sensible Hare and the Case of Carrots
Peter the Penguin Pioneer

Contents

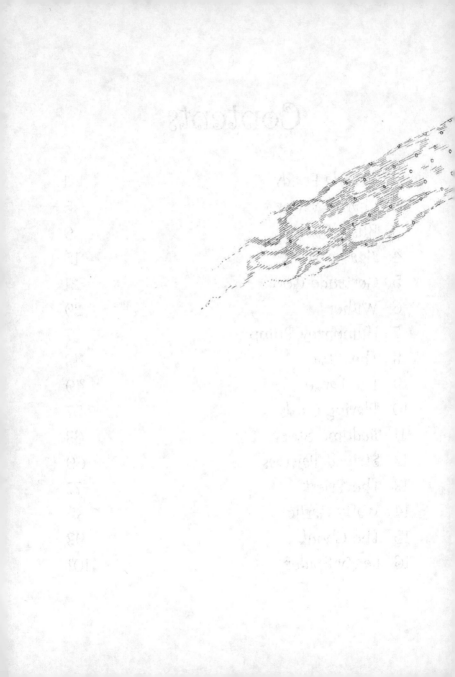

1
Pamela Fraidy

You still-alives are so mean to us ghosties. Only yesterday you locked Pamela Fraidy in the attic. She's a nervous wreck as it is! Not all ghosties can pass through walls, you know. That's only in cartoons and storybooks.

The only ghosty who can pass through walls is Charlie Vapor. He can pass through ceilings too, even when he's wearing a hat.

Poor Pamela. We could hear her shivering from outside the attic door.

"Try to keep calm," I told her through the

1

wood. "We'll get you out."

"Help!" Pamela cried. "It's d-d-dark in here, and I think it may be haunted."

I asked Charlie to pass through into the attic, to comfort her.

"Certainly not, Tabitha," said Charlie, in that adorable cockney accent of his. "It would be an invasion of her privacy."

"But she's petrified."

"Who isn't? This rickety old house gives me the shivers. No wonder the still-alives always look flustered."

"Charlie," I said, "please do comfort Pamela." Charlie passed his head through the door, then pulled it out quickly. "It's dark in there. I reckon I'll wait out here with you, Tabitha."

"But you're the only ghosty who can pass through."

Once again, Charlie passed his head through the door, shuddered, and pulled it back out.

"Tabitha Tumbly, I refuse to float into that attic. There's a spider in there as big as my hat."

Pamela was getting desperate. "What are you *doing* out there?"

"Don't you worry about a thing," I told her.

"We will float downstairs and fetch the key." That happened yesterday, and the key is still on the hook by the front door. The problem is, ghosties can't pick things up.

I can move things. I'm a poltergeist. That's why they call me Tabitha Tumbly. To be honest, I'm not very good at it. I can make a basket of laundry tumble off the sideboard, or an orange roll along the kitchen table, but I can't lift a key from a hook, float it upstairs, and insert it into a keyhole. Only a still-alive can do that. But, as Wither would put it, you still-alives are mean.

2

Charlie Vapor

Charlie and I left Pamela Fraidy quivering in the attic and wisped downstairs to the hall, where we found Wither floating by the hat stand.

"Where are the still-alives when we need them?" Charlie asked him.

"The still-alives are frightfully mean," said Wither, wrinkling his forehead. "You're better off without them."

"We need them to help us with the key," I told him.

"They won't help," said Charlie as the three

5

of us floated toward the front door. "It was the still-alives who locked Pamela in the attic in the first place."

"They didn't intend to."

Wither folded his bony arms. "Tabitha, they were being mean, and you know it."

"Even so," I said, "it doesn't hurt to ask."

"There's a still-alive in here," said Charlie, passing his head through the wall.

"I haven't been in that room since I was still alive," I said. "Which room is it?"

"It's the drawing room," said Wither.

"The drawing room?"

"He means the lounge," said Charlie. "Wither is frightfully old-fashioned."

"I call it the living room," I said. "At least, I did when I was still living."

"Life was more civilized in my day," said Charlie. He took off his hat—it's the polite thing to do—and passed through the lounge wall.

A moment later, we heard a loud scream, and Charlie reappeared white as a, um, ghost. "Those still-alives give me the shivers."

"Any luck?"

"No, Tabitha. There was one sitting in an armchair eating corn flakes. I bid her good morning, and she picked up her breakfast tray and threw it at me."

"Perhaps she wasn't hungry."

Wither frowned. "Why are the still-alives so mean?"

"I told you they wouldn't help," said Charlie, putting his hat back on. "We'll have to move the key ourselves. Tabitha, you can move objects."

"Oh, not terribly well."

"Don't be modest. You're a poltergeist."

"I could try." I closed my eyes, then opened them again.

"No. I simply cannot do it."

"Try again."

I tried, and the key jiggled.

"You must think I'm a frightful show-off."

"Not at all," said Charlie and Wither together.

"I'm sorry," Wither said to Charlie, "I didn't mean to talk over you."

"No," said Charlie, "it was I who spoke over you. Tabitha, do try again."

"Face the other way," I said. "I can't do it with you two watching."

Charlie and Wither turned to the wall.

"No peeking." I gave the key a good jiggle. It jiggled and jingled and jangled, but stubbornly refused to move from the hook.

"It isn't your fault," said Wither.

"Don't blame yourself," Charlie said, adjusting his tie. "The hook is an awkward shape."

3
Rusty Chains

We floated about for a bit, and then Charlie had an idea. "There is only one ghosty who can free the key from that hook, and that ghosty is Rusty Chains."

Every ghosty has a ghostly ability. Rusty Chains has the ability to make things old and rusty. He also has the ability to bore a ghosty to tears. He drags these heavy chains around, so it takes him forever to do anything.

"I'll wisp away and find him," said Wither.

"Charlie should go," I said. "He's the only

ghosty who can pass through."

"Not sure I can," said Charlie, and he blushed bright white.

"You just passed through the lounge door."

"It was a very thin door, Tabitha."

"Charlie Vapor," I said, "this is no time for false modesty. Pamela is locked in the attic with a leggy spider, and we three are floating around doing nothing."

Charlie adjusted his tie. "Perhaps I shall pass through a teeny bit. Not enough to show off, just enough to find Rusty."

Wither was losing his patience. "Oh, get on with it!"

Charlie removed his hat—it's the polite thing to do—and poked his head through the tiled floor. "Rusty? Coo-ee! Has any ghosty seen Rusty Chains? Ah, Rusty. Would you mind floating up here to help us?"

It took Rusty one hour to drag his chains up

the cellar stairs and another hour to drag them along the hallway to the front door.

"Is this it?" asked Rusty Chains, eyeing the hook.

We nodded our ghostly heads.

"I can't do it now. I have to float back down to the cellar, then jangle my chains and moan a lot."

Wither folded his bony arms. "But it took you two hours to get here. How long does it take to

dab a bit of rust on a hook?"

"Anything for a quiet life," moaned Rusty, rattling his chains noisily.

"Just the hook," said Charlie. "We don't want to damage the key."

Rusty dabbed the hook with his rusty chains. The hook turned brown and crumbled to dust, and the key chinked onto the tiles.

"How did you keep the rust off the key?" asked Charlie.

"I didn't think about it. I just jangled my chains and moaned a lot."

"You miserable old moaner!"

"Charlie," said Wither, "don't be mean. Rusty, we are grateful for your help."

"Thank you, Rusty," I said. "Charlie, are you going to thank Rusty?"

Charlie removed his hat—it's the polite thing to do—replaced it on his head, and shook Rusty Chains by the hand.

4

Agatha Draft

"We're not out of the woods yet," I said.

"No," said Charlie. "And Pamela Fraidy is still not out of the attic. She's probably been eaten by the leggy spider."

"Spiders don't eat ghosties," said Wither. "Spiders are mean, but they're not *that* mean. I will float upstairs and ask how she is." And off he wisped.

"We need to move the key along the hallway and up the stairs, Charlie," I said.

"If we wait long enough, Tabitha, perhaps a

still-alive will walk down the hall and kick the key to the foot of the staircase."

I shook my haunted head. "The still-alive is just as likely to hide the key in his pocket."

"Can't you jiggle it across the floor?"

"I haven't the skills. What if I jiggle it wrong, and it floats out through the letterbox and jangles off up the street? Ah, here's Wither."

"That was quick," said Charlie.

"I bumped into Headless Lesley on the staircase," said Wither. "He'd just been up to the attic and held his head to the keyhole. It was too dark to see much, he said, but she seemed to be in good spirits."

"Perhaps we should ask Agatha Draft," said Charlie, toying with the brim of his trilby hat. "She could create an eerie breeze and blow the key all the way to the foot of the staircase."

"Poor Aggie," said Wither. "The still-alives are so mean to her. Have you seen the way they hunch their shoulders when she floats past?"

"When I last saw her," I said, "she was in the dining room. Let's float in and say hello."

And off we wisped.

The dining room door was open, so we floated straight in.

Three still-alives were sitting shivering at the dining table. Agatha Draft was floating behind their heads, blowing their hair without a care. When she saw us ghosties, she billowed the curtains for a bit and then wisped over to say hello.

"Tabitha Tumbly, Wither, how the devil are you? Charlie, how lovely to see you."

"This is no time for pleasantries," said Charlie. "Pamela Fraidy is locked in the attic with a leggy spider."

"Poor Pamela!" gasped Agatha. "What can we do-woo-whooo?"

On hearing Agatha's concerned cry, the still-alives leapt from their chairs and ran about. The two half-sized still-alives hid beneath the table, playing a game I suppose, and the still-alive with the high heels began to scream.

"Never mind them," said Wither. "They're just mean."

"It's frightfully rude," said Charlie as the four of us floated out to the hall. "Agatha, will you help?"

"You could create a draft," I said, "and blow the key down the hall to the foot of the staircase."

"We saw the way you billowed those curtains," said Charlie. "Awfully impressive."

"You must think I'm the most ghastly show-off."

"Not at all," we all said together. Then I apologized for talking over Charlie, and Charlie apologized for talking over me, and then Wither apologized for talking over us both.

"Had I known you were watching," said Agatha, clutching her pearls modestly, "I would

have billowed with a little more discretion."

We floated up the hall to the front door, to where the key lay on the tiles.

"This is frightfully embarrassing," said Agatha.

"We're not watching," I said, and the three of us turned to face the front door.

A moment later we heard a clatter, and when we turned around, Agatha was blushing bright white and the key was at the far end of the hall, at the foot of the staircase.

Wither, Charlie, and I clapped our haunted hands.

"It is a very *small* key," said Agatha.

5
Gertrude Goo

"All we have to do now," said Charlie Vapor, "is get the key up the staircase, then up the three rickety steps to the attic door."

We looked at the staircase, at the varnished banister, and at the plushly carpeted stairs. And suddenly it seemed that there were an awful lot of stairs and that the top stair was teeteringly high.

"How many stairs are there, Tabitha?"

"I don't know, Charlie. At my school we used calculators."

Wither frowned. "Our math teacher used to whack our knuckles with a ruler. Thwack!"

"Wither had a classical education," said Charlie.

"That is correct. Latin, Shakespeare, Dickens. We learned by rote."

I looked at Charlie. "What does he mean, 'by rote'?"

"I don't know, Tabitha. At my school we learned to tap dance." He removed his hat—the polite thing to do—and performed an elegant little jig.

And that was when Gertrude Goo floated into view. "While you three ghosties are making merry, poor Pamela Fraidy is locked in the attic. The leggy spider keeps scampering about, and she's a nervous wreck as it is."

"We were counting the stairs," Charlie told her.

"I know this house inside out. I clean it from

bottom to top twice daily." Gertrude tickled the banister with her gooey feather duster. "There are twenty-six steps in this house. The front doorstep, the back doorstep, nine steps down to the cellar, twelve stairs here, and the three steps up to the attic door."

When Gertrude was still alive, she worked at the house as a housekeeper. This is why she is so house proud. She spends most of the day straightening pictures and flicking her icky feather duster. The trouble is, she leaves a trail of glowing blue goo wherever she goes.

"How do we lift the key up twelve steps?" wondered Charlie.

"That's easy," I said. "We ask the still-alives to carry it up."

"They won't help us," said Wither, folding his bony arms. "You know how mean they are, particularly the one with the beard."

"We could drop it in one of these shoes," said

23

Charlie, admiring a pair of black leather oxfords. "The still-alive will put the shoes on and walk it up."

I shook my head. "The key would smell of wafty socks."

"We could stick the key to the sole," Charlie said, "with Gertrude's goo."

"We'd have to turn the shoe on its side." Wither rubbed his bristly chin. "What if we apply the goo to the key and then wait for a still-alive to step on it?"

We all looked at Gertrude.

"Don't look at me," said Gertrude, waving the duster, spraying goo onto the carpet, ceiling, and walls. "I don't have any goo. I'm awfully fastidious." And she floated off up the hall to the front door.

"The house would be cleaner if she spent the day in bed," whispered Charlie Vapor.

Wither pursed his lips. "Don't be mean."

"Ah, here comes a still-alive," said Charlie as we heard the click of high heels. "Miss, would you mind awfully—"

The still-alive screamed and ran back into the lounge.

Wither's lip quivered. "How can they be so mean?"

"I should have removed my hat," said Charlie Vapor, and we agreed that that would have been the polite thing to do.

"If you don't mind," said Gertrude, floating back along the hall toward us, "I have to finish my chores. The house won't clean itself, you know."

"Gertrude," said Charlie, "would you mind applying a dollop of goo—"

"Charlie," I whispered, "Gertrude prides herself on her cleanliness. She would never admit to making a mess. We will have to trick her."

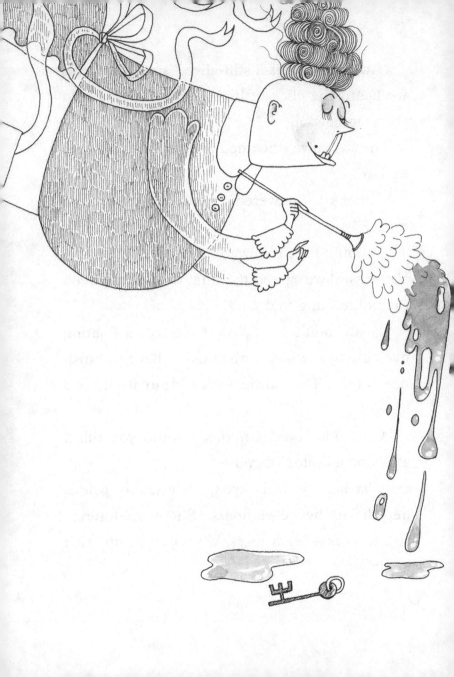

Charlie gave me a knowing wink. "Gerty," he said, taking off his hat, "this key is frightfully dusty. Would you mind giving it a quick spruce?"

"All in a day's work," said Gertrude, waving her feather duster.

It took Gertrude ten minutes to polish that key. By the time she wisped off, the key was as sticky as a bug in a bag of sticky toffee.

6
Wither

We didn't have to wait long. The big bearded still-alive walked out of the kitchen, a mug of coffee in his hand, and stepped directly onto the gooey key.

We floated up to the ceiling to hide. Me, Charlie Vapor, and Wither.

"What if the still-alive doesn't walk up the stairs?" Charlie asked, adjusting his cuff links.

The moment he said this, the still-alive turned and went back into the kitchen, slamming the door behind him, the key stuck gooily to his shoe.

"Perhaps," said Wither, "he forgot the milk."

"Or the sugar," I said.

Charlie Vapor passed through the kitchen door, the show-off, then passed back. "Yes, Tabitha, he's fetched himself a generous heap of sugar, and he's giving it a stir."

Wither frowned.

The kitchen door opened again, and we floated up out of sight.

"I hope the still-alive walks upstairs," I said. We floated about for a bit, and Charlie dropped his hat—not a polite thing to do—but still the still-alive remained in the hall.

"Perhaps we could *ask* it to walk upstairs," said Wither.

"Charlie," I said, "you ask. You have such frightfully good manners. Well, for a cockney."

Charlie started to float down, but then he floated back up. "Shall I remove my hat?"

"It's the polite thing to do," I said.

And down he floated.

But then he floated back up. "I don't want to appear too formal, you see."

"It's good to be polite, Charlie."

Again, Charlie floated down. This time, he wisped over to the still-alive and doffed his trilby hat. "Awfully sorry to trouble you, and I hate to be a bother—"

"Please don't be mean to us," said Wither, floating down behind him.

The still-alive yelped, threw the mug of coffee across the hall and ran up the staircase, the key still stuck to his shoe. "Aaah!" he cried.

"Aaaaah!"

"How frightfully kind of you," said Charlie, as we followed the still-alive up the staircase. "We wouldn't have asked, only—"

"Help!"

"Pamela Fraidy is locked in the attic," I said, "with a leggy spider, and—"

"Oh, please help me!"

"And spiders are mean and horrid," Wither added, covering his eyes with his hands.

"Please, no!"

The key dropped from the shoe two steps from the top.

"Thanks awfully," said Charlie Vapor.

The still-alive ran into a bedroom at the front of the house and slammed the door. Charlie passed through, then passed back. "It must be frightfully cold in those rooms, Tabitha. He's shivering and shouting, and he has pulled the bedcovers right over his head."

"Never mind that," I said. "We have to lift the key up the top two stairs, then up the three creaky wooden steps to the attic."

Charlie adjusted his tie. "You can do that, Tabitha Tumbly. You're the poltergeist."

"Hardly," I said. "I can topple the odd bottle."

"Don't be modest. We saw the way you jiggled the key. If you can jiggle it, you can lift it."

"Not with you two watching."

"We're not watching—are we, Wither?"

And the two ghosties turned to face the wall. I was just about to lift the key when Pamela Fraidy shouted through the attic door. "Will you get on with it? I'm locked in the attic with a leggy spider, and I'm a nervous wreck as it is."

"Certainly," I said. But then I heard a blub.

"Wither," I said, touching him on the shoulder, "whatever is the matter?"

"Oh, Tabitha! Why do ghosties have to be so mean?"

"No one is being mean, Wither."

"Pamela told us off. I hate being told off." Wither rubbed his eyes with his hands. "Tabitha, will you ask Pamela to stop being mean?"

I floated up to the attic door and peered through the keyhole. "Pamela? Pamela dear, are you still there? Have you been eaten by the leggy spider?"

"I'm here, Tabitha. Wither is right. There is no excuse for meanness."

"You've been under a lot of pressure, Pamela."

"It's just so frightfully dark in here, and what with the leggy spider—" I heard a faint, eerie sob. "Tabitha, please apologize to Wither on my behalf."

I floated back down the three rickety wooden steps and rejoined Wither and Charlie at the top of the staircase. "Wither, Pamela says—"

"This key won't lift itself," said Charlie Vapor.

"Face the wall," I said, "and I'll see what I can do."

Charlie and Wither turned away. I lifted the key and fitted it into the lock.

7

Humphrey Bump

"You were marvelous, darling, marvelous," Charlie said, clapping his hands. "We're awfully impressed."

"All I did was lift the key—"

"You fitted it into the lock, Tabitha. No other ghosty could have done that."

"Charlie, you can pass through walls."

He shrugged. "Bricks and mortar, Tabitha."

"I can't do anything," said Wither, and his bottom lip trembled. "All I do is blub and tremble and flit about."

"But you're in touch with your feelings," I told him. "What a wonderful quality to possess."

"You should write poetry, Wither," said Charlie, and he looked at me and winked.

"Actually, I do write poetry."

"There," I said. "You *can* do something."

"My poems won't get Pamela out of the attic."

"You could write a poem about key turning," said Charlie.

"And how would that help?"

We heard Pamela Fraidy clear her throat.

"Er-herm! If you three wouldn't mind—"

"We'll have you out in the turn of a key," said Charlie Vapor. "Tabitha?"

"Avert your gaze, and I will see what I can do."

"That's the spirit," said Charlie Vapor. He turned to face the wall—the polite thing to do—and Wither buried his eyes in his bottom lip.

"It's no good," I said, jiggling the key. "I can

turn the key, but the door needs a push."

"We could ask Humphrey Bump to bump into it," said Charlie Vapor.

Humphrey is the sort of ghosty who can bump into still-alives, then wisp away the moment they turn round. He can bump into doors, furniture, and household pets.

"That bumbling schoolboy won't help," said

Wither. "You know how mean-spirited he is."

"We could ask him nicely," I said.

Wither bit his fingernails nervously. "I could read him one of my poems, in payment."

"That's a lovely

idea," I said. "I saw him bobbing about in the back bedroom. Wither, do float in and fetch him."

"I don't mean to be rude," Charlie whispered as Wither wisped away, "but Wither's poems are drivel."

To our shivery surprise, when Wither floated out from the bedroom, Humphrey was floating beside him.

Humphrey wisped into position, and I gave the key a twist. But Humphrey just bobbed about, his hands in his blazer pockets. "I can't do it with everybody watching."

"Let's give the boy some privacy," said Charlie. "After all, it is the polite thing to do." He adjusted his hat, then followed Wither into the back bedroom.

I turned the key, Humphrey bumped, the bolt unbolted, the attic door creaked open, and out wisped Pamela. "Thank heavens for that!"

I shook Humphrey by the hand. "Awfully kind of you to help."

"I didn't have much choice," Humphrey said. "Wither threatened to read me one of his poems."

8
The Attic

Humphrey pulled a ghostly lollipop from his pocket and offered it to Pamela Fraidy.

"I'm sweet enough as it is," said Pamela, "but thanks awfully."

"How did you end up locked in the attic?" Humphrey asked.

"I floated in to say hello to one of the still-alives, the one with the adorable high heels. She was sorting through a box of crockery. She let out a frightful shriek, dashed out, and slammed the door in my face."

"Yes," I said. "I witnessed the whole thing. She locked the attic door and ran downstairs with the key."

"No wonder I'm a nervous wreck," said Pamela. "There's a spider in that attic as big as Charlie's hat. Perhaps we could stamp on it."

Charlie looked horrified. "Stamp on my trilby? You will do no such thing."

"Not your hat, Charlie. The leggy spider. Or perhaps Humphrey could bump into it."

Humphrey gave the lollipop a ghostly lick, then shook his head.

"You're a coward," said Charlie, "like Pamela."

"That was double mean," said Wither. "You were mean to Pamela, *and* you were mean to Humphrey."

Charlie removed his hat. "Pamela, please accept my sincere and hatless apology."

"You have to apologize to Humphrey too," said Wither. "With your hat off."

"He wears that hat only because he's going bald," said Humphrey, giving the lollipop another lick.

"Will the meanness never end?" cried Wither, and he wisped down the staircase to the hall.

Pamela was deep in thought. "I have an idea. Charlie, you could trap the leggy spider in your hat."

"A spider in a trilby is still a spider," said Charlie.

"Trap it in the hat, then tip the spider out of the window."

"Worth a try," Charlie said, "but it's awfully dark in that attic. Tabitha, light the candle."

"I'm not sure I have the skills, Charlie."

"Tabitha, if you can't light that candle, I'll eat my hat."

I floated into the attic, lit the candle—it was nothing, really—and floated out. "I couldn't see the spider. It must have scampered away."

"Leave this to me," Charlie said, adjusting his tie. He checked the floorboards, the wooden beams, and the brickwork. The candle flickered, and the wind howled, but there was no leggy spider to be found.

"I think it scampered in here," said Pamela, and she wisped into the study.

The still-alive in the high heels was seated at the desk, typing on the clicky-clacky typewriter. When she saw Pamela, she screamed and ran out of the room, slamming the study door behind her.

"Oh, that's done it!" cried Charlie. "We've only just rescued Pamela from the attic, and now she's shut in the study."

"Can't Humphrey just bump the door open?" I asked.

"Not a chance," said Charlie. "This door opens outward."

Wither came floating back up the staircase.

"The muse has struck. I have a poem in my head, and I just *have* to write it down. Where's my quivery quill?"

"In the study," I said. "With the leggy spider. And Pamela. One of the still-alives shut her in."

"This really is the limit," said Charlie Vapor.

"He's right," I said. "The still-alives have gone too far. Something must be done."

We heard Pamela Fraidy's voice vibrate through the wood. "You have to get me out. This room is far smaller than the attic. The leggy spider is scampering about, and I'm a nervous wreck as it is."

"Pamela," said Wither, floating close to the study door, "I have an idea."

We all wisped round to listen.

"I will dictate the poem through the door. Pamela, you will need quill, parchment, and ink."

9
The Larder

While Wither dictated his poem, Charlie floated off down the staircase, his trilby held thoughtfully to his chest.

I wanted to know where he was going, so I wisped down the stairs to join him. "Charlie, where are you floating off to?"

"The larder, for a private think."

"What about?"

"We need to call a meeting, Tabitha. I need to think of a time when we will all be together. We ghosties are so frightfully busy."

"I'll come with you."

"I think better alone, Tabitha."

"Me too," I said.

Just as we were floating in through the kitchen door, Wither wisped down the staircase toward us. "Where are you two floating off to?"

"The larder, for a private think," Charlie said.

"Just the two of us," I said. "We think better alone."

Wither pursed his lips. He looked like he was chewing a wasp. "You don't want me around?"

Charlie shook his head.

"Well," said Wither, "as long as I know where I float." And he floated off across the kitchen.

"Wither," I said, floating after him, "where are you going?"

"The larder." He floated in through the larder

door.

Charlie and I were about to float in after him when Humphrey Bump bobbed by. "What are you three up to?"

"We're floating into the larder," I told him, "for a private think."

"I'll join you," Humphrey said, licking his lollipop.

"If you must," said Wither, peering out from the larder. "Though I have to say, we think better alone."

Charlie was about to protest when we heard a rattling sound, followed by a low moan.

"It's coming from the larder," said Humphrey.

"Rusty," I said, floating in through the larder door, "what are you doing here?"

"I want to be alone," said Rusty Chains, and he gave his chains a good old rattle.

I was about to explain that the larder was a place for quiet contemplation when I heard a voice from above. It was Agatha Draft. "How is a ghosty supposed to concentrate with all that rattling?"

"Agatha," Charlie said, floating up to the larder ceiling, "wisp out of here at once."

"I'd rather not," said Agatha, clutching her pearls. "Gertrude and I are engaged in conversation."

"That is, we were until you lot floated in," Gertrude said.

"I came in here to be alone," Charlie said, not removing his hat. "All I want to do is float up and down, scratch the top of my head, and think."

"What about?" asked Agatha.

"We need to call a meeting. I need to think of a time when we will all be together. We ghosties are so frightfully busy."

"We're all together now," Humphrey said, bobbing in through the larder door.

Charlie rubbed his chin. "I rather suppose we are."

"What is the meeting to be about?" asked Wither.

"The still-alives."

Wither frowned. "But they're mean!"

"That is what the meeting is about. Their mean behavior, and how to stop it."

"We could make friends with them," I said. "Then they won't be mean to us. People aren't mean to their friends."

"My friends are mean to me," said Wither.

"I have invented three rules," Charlie said. "If we follow these three rules, the still-alives will like us, and they won't keep shutting Pamela in rooms."

"Right," I said. "What's the first rule?"

"Every day, we say hello to the still-alives. It's the polite thing to do, and it will put the still-alives in a pleasant mood. The rule is called

Rule Three because there are three rules. Any questions?"

Wither raised a pale hand. "What's the second rule?"

"I was just coming to that. Each night, we tell the still-alives a bedtime story."

"Everyone loves a good story," said Agatha Draft. "What is this second rule called?"

"It's called Rule One because it is one of the rules. Is every ghosty with me on this?"

We nodded our haunted heads.

Wither raised his other hand. "I don't wish to be mean, Charlie, but you promised three rules, and there appear to be only two. Is there a third rule?"

"I was just coming to that. No floating at night. It gives the still-alives the creeps. I have no idea why. We call this Rule Two, because there are two other rules."

"I'm not sure that makes sense," said Wither,

"but that's what we've come to expect from you, Charlie Vapor."

Charlie folded his arms. "Now who's being mean?"

10
Playing Cards

When we gathered in the hall the following day, Wither was dressed for bed. He was wearing blue-and-white striped pajamas and a floppy nightcap.

Charlie laughed. "Are you tired, Wither?"

"I thought we were doing Rule Three."

"Rule Three," I said, "is the rule where we say hello to the still-alives."

"That's right," said Charlie. "Are we all here? Ah, here's Gertrude and Aggie. Anyone heard from Rusty?"

"Had to cancel," I said. "Something about ten billion years in purgatory."

"We can't wait that long. We'll have to start without him. Humphrey, would you mind very much?"

Humphrey bumped the lounge door. It swung open, and we floated in.

Two still-alives, the bearded one and the one with the high heels, were seated at a card table, playing a game of cards.

I myself am terribly shy, but Charlie wisped up to them, bold as brass, took off his hat—the polite thing to do—and bid them a good day.

The still-alives were so surprised that the bearded one dropped his cards and dived beneath the table, and the other dashed across the room and hid behind the curtains.

"Perhaps we should have knocked," said Charlie Vapor.

"We came to say hello," said Wither. "We want

to make friends with you so you'll stop being mean."

"Let me tidy these cards," said Gertrude Goo, but all she could do was float above them, dripping a trail of glowing blue goo.

From under the table, the bearded still-alive screamed.

"Don't be cross with Gertrude," said Charlie. "She was trying to help. Humphrey, offer him a lick of your lollipop."

Humphrey tried to float under the table, but he kept bumping into it, bump bump bump, until it toppled on to its side.

The still-alive rolled into a ball and pulled the rug over his head.

"The poor dear is shivering," said Agatha breezily. "It is cold in here, what with that open window."

"Perhaps he wants us to play cards with him," I said.

"I used to be a professional poker player," said Charlie, "when I was still alive. Who will deal? Tabitha?"

I dealt the cards as well as I could, but the deal turned into more of a shuffle. A midair shuffle.

The cards ended up all over the carpet.

"Um, nothing up my sleeve," I said, then floated off to the window, where the high-heeled still-alive had wrapped herself in the curtain.

"No need to be shy. I'm shy myself, but I don't let it bother me. Would you say so, Wither?"

"You're right," said Wither, wisping across the room. "Though you do talk to curtains, which is the first sign of madness."

"I'm not talking to the curtain. I'm talking to the still-alive wrapped inside the curtain."

"Oh, then you must lift the curtain so that the still-alive can hear."

"I would, had I the skills."

"Perhaps," said Wither, "we can ask Agatha to billow it."

"Aggie?" I called, and across the room she wisped. "Dear Aggie! That's the spirit. Terribly decent of you. Would you mind very much?"

"Avert your gaze, then. Billowing makes one

blush."

Wither and I turned away, and Agatha blew up the most ferocious gale, and when we looked again, the still-alive had gone.

"Oh dear," said Agatha, clutching her pearls shamefully. "I billowed too hard, and I blew the still-alive out of the window."

11

Bedtime Story

Wither kept his pajamas on all day. "There's no point dressing now," he would say whenever a ghosty spookily sniggered. "I'd just put on the second sock, and it would be bedtime."

We spent most of the day trying to free Pamela Fraidy from the study, but the door wouldn't budge. Poor Pamela. No wonder she was a nervous wreck.

When the still-alives went to bed, we gathered on the landing, and Charlie announced that it was time for Rule One. "Are we all here? Still no sign of Rusty. Has anyone heard from Headless Lesley?"

"He has a headache," said Humphrey. "He dropped it."

"Which rule is Rule One?" asked Gertrude Goo.

"Rule One," I said, "is the rule where we read the still-alives a bedtime story."

"Everyone loves a good story," said Agatha.

"Humphrey," Charlie said, floating toward one of the front bedrooms, "bump this door open, and we'll get started."

Humphrey bumped the door, and it opened with a creepy creak. The high-heeled still-alive was sitting at a desk, reading a book. She must have been terribly excited to see us. When we all floated in, her hair stood on end, and she flapped her arms with joy.

"You can put the book away," I said kindly.

"We're here to tell you a story."

"Everyone loves a good story," said Agatha. The still-alive let out an excited scream.

"Calm down," I told her. "We haven't even started yet."

"Once upon a time," Charlie began, "a still-alive was alone in a rickety old house. Rain lashed against the windows, and the curtains billowed—"

"Like this," said Agatha, billowing the curtains.

"—and six frightfully friendly ghosties wisped down the chimney and said hello," Charlie went on, "and those who were wearing hats took them off, like this." And he removed his hat.

"It's the polite thing to do," I said, in case the still-alive didn't know. Certainly she looked confused. She had her knees up to her chest, and she covered her eyes with her hands.

"My nightcap stays on," said Wither. "I'm bald, Charlie. I get such a cold head."

"Then," Charlie continued, "the ghosties

danced around the still-alive in a spectral circle, like this."

And there we were wisping around the room, faster and faster and faster, whoo-whooo-whooo, and I have to say, the still-alive was not impressed. She pulled her nightie up over her head and pressed her hands to her ears.

"I don't think it likes this story," I said, wisping over to the bookcase. "What kind of stories do you like?"

"Suggest a few titles," said Charlie Vapor. I began taking books from the shelf and showing them to the still-alive. I'm no better at suggesting books than I am at shuffling playing cards. The books ended up flying around the room.

"Perhaps the still-alive doesn't want a bedtime story," said Wither, and the still-alive screamed.

"Everyone loves a good story," said Agatha.

"Not this still-alive," said Charlie, taking off

his hat. "Let's float away."

"But I'm about to read the still-alive a poem," said Wither.

"All the more reason to float away," Charlie said, which was not terribly kind, you have to admit.

12

Striped Pajamas

"I was the first ghosty here," said Wither, when we gathered on the landing late that night. "I was already in my pajamas, you see. The rest of you had to wisp away and change."

"Yes," said Charlie, who was still wearing his trilby, "and you have looked ridiculous all day as a result."

Then we heard Pamela's shaky voice call out through the study door. "I hope you're working on a rescue plan."

"Pamela," I called back, "whenever we get

you out, you get shut in again."

"So you're leaving me in here forever? With the leggy spider? It's scampering about, and I'm a nervous wreck as it is."

"We have to go to bed now, Pamela," Charlie said. "Goodnight."

"But what about the rescue plan?"

"This is part of the rescue plan," Charlie explained, doffing his trilby. "If we make friends with the still-alives, they'll let you out as a gesture of goodwill. We'll retire to the bed in this room here, and we'll let the still-alives get a good night's sleep. Humphrey, bump the door."

The back bedroom was far grander than those at the front. When the door creaked open, we all gasped. The bedroom had an ornate four-poster bed and plush velvet curtains.

"I hope there's enough room for us all," said Agatha Draft. "Who will lift the sheets? Tabitha,

you're a poltergeist. Would you mind awfully?"

"I don't have the skills, Agatha. Billow it with a force ten gale."

"Tabitha dear, I'll be lucky if I can rustle up a gentle breeze."

"Ladies," said Charlie, taking off his hat, "why not both try together?"

We both tried together.

The sheets lifted up, and they bulged like the sail on a pirate ship.

"Well done, Tabitha," said Agatha Draft, clutching her pearls joyfully.

"Agatha, I barely touched it."

"Put your modesty aside," Charlie said, adjusting his trilby, "and come to bed."

"I've not had a good night's sleep since I was still alive," said Gertrude. She crawled into bed, leaving a trail of glowing blue goo.

Charlie floated into bed beside her, and Wither wisped in on Charlie's left and Humphrey to his right, and I floated into the space between Humphrey and Charlie, and then Humphrey bumped us all along to make space for dear Aggie. The blanket came to rest, covering our toes and knees.

"It's drafty here at the edge," said Gertrude.

"You think it's drafty there?" I complained. "You try lying beside Agatha."

"Don't be mean to Agatha," said Wither.

"What about me?" protested Humphrey. "I'm at the edge, *and* I'm beside Agatha."

"Wither has cold feet," said Charlie Vapor.

"Don't be mean," said Wither. "At least I'm not wearing an outdoor hat."

"Shh!" said Agatha. "I can hear someone coming."

Twelve eerie eyeballs turned to the door.

The door creaked open, and there, in striped pajamas not unlike Wither's, stood the bearded still-alive.

"Perhaps he wants to sleep in this bed," blubbed Wither.

"I should have thought of that," whispered Charlie.

The still-alive didn't see us at first. He took a key from his pajama pocket, closed and locked the door, and returned the key to his pocket. It was only as he crept across the rug that he noticed we were here, six grinning ghosties all in a row. He screamed a mean-spirited scream and ran back to the door.

"Awfully sorry," said Agatha, clutching her pearls. "We were trying to keep out of your way."

"We can budge over if you like," said Charlie. "There's plenty of room for all."

"We're trying to make friends with you," I explained.

"Then you will stop being mean to us," added Wither.

The still-alive pulled the key from his pocket so

excitedly that he dropped it onto the floorboards. He leapt up and down for a moment before diving under the bed, headfirst.

"He's trying to find the key," I said. "We should help. That's what friends are for."

We all wisped under the bed.

"It's dark under here," blubbed Wither. There wasn't much room under the bed, so we had to keep wisping out and wisping back under again.

"Help! Help!" the still-alive yelled. Presumably he wanted us to help him find the key.

"It has to be here somewhere," said Agatha, wisping in and out of the still-alive's pajamas.

This went on for several minutes, until finally the still-alive crawled out from under the bed, grabbed the key from where it had rolled beneath the dresser, banged the door several times with his fists, wailed at the top of his lungs, unlocked the door, and ran out.

Not frightfully friendly, I have to say, though he did leave the bedroom door open so we could float on to the landing and say goodnight to poor Pamela.

13

The Priest

Gertrude Goo and I were floating by the lounge ceiling when the doorbell donged.

"Who-woo-whooo could that be?" asked Gertrude, dripping glowing blue goo onto the coffee table.

"Don't ask me," I said. "I don't even live here. I don't live anywhere. I'm not alive, you see."

We floated to the lounge door and listened. First we heard the sound of high heels as one of the still-alives walked down the hall to open the front door. We heard voices for a moment and then the footsteps again, click-click-click, together with the footsteps of the visitor, clump-clump-clump.

"I hope they don't come in here," I said.

Gertrude agreed. "Just look at the place. I'd better tidy up."

I watched as Gertrude floated about the room, tidying pictures, ornaments, the vase of flowers, and the rows and rows of books, spraying the room with glowing blue goo.

"That's quite enough tidying for one day," I told her.

"I'll just give the shelves a quick dusting. I'm terribly house proud, you see."

The door handle turned with a creak.

"Gertrude, there isn't time."

We floated up to the ceiling and wisped into the lampshade to hide. The still-alive entered with the guest, an elderly man dressed in black.

"He's got his shirt on back to front," said

Gertrude.

When the two still-alives saw the goo, their jaws dropped.

"I knew they'd be impressed," said Gertrude. "Tabitha, I do believe he's a priest."

"There is something sinister going on," I said. "Let's tell the others."

We wisped out of the lampshade, out into the hall, and up the staircase to the landing.

Wither was dictating a poem to Pamela through the study door. "When the other ghosties are mean to me, it makes my feelings sway like a tree."

The moment he saw Gertrude and me floating behind him, he blushed bright white.

"This is only the first draft. And talking of drafts, has any ghosty seen Agatha?"

Pamela's voice vibrated through the wood.

"She's in the garden, floating by the clothesline. I can see her through the window."

"We'd better fetch her," I said. "Wither, the still-alives have brought in a priest."

"Perhaps," said Wither, as we floated down the staircase, "the still-alives have discovered religion."

Charlie and Humphrey were floating by the stove, watching Agatha through the kitchen window.

"Agatha is drying the still-alives' laundry," said Charlie Vapor, "as a gesture of goodwill."

"We must fetch her," I said. "The still-alives have brought in a priest."

"A priest?" said Agatha, wisping in through the open window. "We must say hello."

"It's the polite thing to do," said Charlie, lifting his hat.

And off we floated to the lounge.

The still-alives were there together now, the Priest, the still-alive with the beard, the still-alive with the high heels, and the two half-sized still-alives. When we wisped in, they hid behind the sofa, all except for the Priest, who was engrossed in a leather-bound book.

"Perhaps they're planning a surprise party," said Wither. "They'll jump out and yell boo!"

"I didn't think priests liked parties," said Charlie.

"Everyone loves a party," said Agatha Draft.

The Priest ran his finger along the mantelpiece and wiped it on his handkerchief. He then reached into his trouser pocket and took out a wooden cross.

"What does the cross mean?" asked Humphrey.

"I think," blubbed Wither, "it means he's cross."

The Priest held the cross in the air, half-closed his eyes, and muttered something we couldn't quite hear.

"He's trying to convert us to religion," said Charlie.

"It's a bit late for that," said Wither. "We're dead."

"Let's float in and explain," I said, but as we floated in, the Priest reached into his other trouser pocket and took out a small white thing, which he then waved about.

"Garlic," observed Charlie.

"I hate garlic," said Wither. "I liked it when I was still alive, but these days I find it abhorrent."

"I don't think any of us ghosties like it," I said. We watched in horror as the Priest peeled the garlic bulb, separated it into cloves, and placed them in different corners of the room.

"Garlic is related to the onion," said Agatha. "Did you know that, Wither?"

"Onion makes me blub."

"Everything makes you blub," said Charlie, and we floated out into the hall.

14

Wafty Garlic

"I don't like this one bit," said Agatha Draft, floating by the lawn mower.

"It's our house too," said Gertrude Goo.

"The entire house wafts of garlic," said Wither, pinching his nose.

Pamela Fraidy wisped out of the study window and floated down to join us. "Thank heavens for that," she said. "I thought they'd never let me out."

"We'd forgotten about you," said Humphrey, bumping into the garden shed.

Wither gave him a withering look. "Don't be mean to Pamela. She's been shut in the study since Tuesday."

"With the leggy spider," added Agatha. "Pamela, how did you open the study window?"

"One of the still-alives opened it. She came in to fetch something, and I wisped into the typewriter to hide. It was the still-alive with the high heels." Pamela rolled her eyes. "Those shoes are to-die-for! She had another still-alive with her. He had his shirt on backward. Must have dressed in the dark."

"The Priest," I said to the others knowingly.

"He placed garlic cloves around the room," Pamela went on. "Nailed an entire bulb to the door."

"The meanness of it all!" cried Wither.

"I wouldn't have minded," said Pamela, "only, I can't stand the smell."

"Garlic does tend to waft," said Agatha,

clutching her pearls.

"The still-alives don't like it much either," said Pamela. "That's why they opened the study window. Why put garlic in a study?"

"It's not just the study," I said. "They're placing it all around the house. Charlie has gone to investigate. We sent Charlie because he's the only ghosty who can pass through. Good old Charlie Vapor!"

"I wish I had a skill," said Wither.

"You can write abysmal poems," said Humphrey Bump.

"Oh, how mean!"

"I think your poems are delightful," I said, though honestly, I thought they were drivel.

"I don't want to write poems," said Wither. "Who reads poems these days? I want to float through walls like Charlie, or blow leaves across the lawn like dear Agatha."

"You can blub," said Humphrey.

"Oh!" cried Wither, and he floated off for a blub.

"This is no time for blubbing," I said. "Here's Charlie."

"That house wafts to high heaven. They've nailed garlic cloves to every door in the house."

"Perhaps they're expecting vampires," Wither said, floating back. "Garlic wards off evil forces."

"The leggy spider didn't seem to mind garlic," said Pamela.

"Spiders don't have noses," said Humphrey.

"Oh yes?" said Wither. "Then how do they smell?"

Humphrey laughed. "Terrible."

Wither shook his head.

"Don't make jokes about spiders," said Pamela. "I'm a nervous wreck as it is, and now the house is riddled with garlic."

"I could tidy it away," offered Gertrude.

"Tabitha, you could float it out of the window,"

said Charlie, adjusting his cuff links.

"They've nailed it to the doors. I'm a poltergeist, not a carpenter. Have they opened any more windows?"

"Only the study window and the lounge," Charlie said.

"How can the still-alives stand the waft?"

"They've put clothespins on their noses, Tabitha. If only we could do that."

"We can," said Gertrude. "I use ghostly clothespins to hang out the ghostly garters. And the spooky bloomers. Oh, and Wither's long johns."

"Wither's long johns waft almost as much as the garlic," said Humphrey Bump.

"Don't be mean to my long johns. If I don't wear long johns, my knees knock."

We floated about by the garden fence for a bit, feeling the breeze blow through our transparent bits. Then Charlie had an idea.

"Our attempt at befriending the still-alives has failed. We need to get them out of the house. The only way to do that is to scare them out."

"We can't scare the still-alives," I told him. "We're too friendly."

Charlie adjusted his hat. "Then there is only one thing for it. We call in a professional."

15
The Ghoul

The following afternoon, Wither and I were floating about in the lounge when we heard a ghostly tap at the window.

"Who could that be?" I asked, looking at Wither. My voice sounded odd because of the clothespin.

"It could be the Ghoul," said Wither. "We hired one, remember?"

I peered out through the lace curtains. "I forgot we'd hired the Ghoul. This must be him. He's ugly enough."

"Oh, don't be mean. Open the window, before he gets cross."

"I'm not sure I have the skills."

"Try," said Wither. "Lift the latch."

"Not with you watching."

Wither covered his eyes with his haunted hands, and I gave the latch a jaunty jiggle.

"There. That's the best I can do."

"Wait here, Tabitha. I'll float off and fetch Humphrey. Perhaps he can bump it."

The moment Wither had gone, I flung the window wide open and invited the Ghoul inside.

A minute later, Wither returned with Humphrey Bump, followed by Charlie Vapor, Pamela Fraidy, Gertrude Goo, and Agatha Draft, each with a clothespin on the nose.

"Would you like a clothespin for your nose, Wither?" Gertrude asked.

"I can't smell a thing with this cold. Tabitha, how did you open the window?"

"One of the still-alives opened it. Everyone, this is the Ghoul."

"Hello, Ghoul," said everyone.

The Ghoul chewed the tip of his nose, and he said nothing.

"This chap will scare the pants off those still-alives," I said cheerfully.

Wither looked doubtful. "But what about the Priest?"

"The Ghoul eats priests for breakfast."

"And what about the Priest's wooden cross?"

"The Ghoul will use the Priest's wooden cross as a toothpick."

"And the garlic?"

"We can take a holler-day," suggested Agatha, clutching her pearls. "When we float back, the garlic will have been eaten by rats."

Charlie passed his head through the lounge door. "I can hear footsteps."

We all floated to the lounge door to listen.

First we heard the click-click-click of high heels, followed by the clump-clump-clump of the Priest and the different-sounding footsteps of the two half-sized still-alives and the still-alive with the beard.

"Let's hide in the lampshade," said Pamela.

"I'm not sharing a lampshade with the Ghoul," said Wither. "He might salivate on me."

"And he's awfully big," said Charlie. "I think he's grown."

Charlie was right. The Ghoul had been able to fit through the window. Now, the Ghoul was the size of a wardrobe.

"Let's wisp up out of the way," said Agatha, "and let the Ghoul get to work."

"It's the polite thing to do," said Charlie, and every ghosty floated up to the ceiling.

That is, every ghosty except for me. I wisped beneath the Ghoul's left eyelid. I wanted to get a Ghoul's eye view. And I have to say, the Ghoul put on quite a performance.

When the still-alives opened the lounge door, he bared his teeth, rolled his eyeballs, flared his nostrils, wagged his tongue, licked his lips, dribbled, and let out the most horrendous, horrifying howl.

The still-alives didn't like this one bit. Ghosties they could tolerate—after all, we're frightfully friendly—but a ghastly ghoul is quite different. All five ran down the hall to the front door. The high-heeled still-alive kicked off her shoes and ran barefoot into the street, followed by the two half-sized still-alives and the Priest. The bearded still-alive was the only still-alive who remained inside.

Ten minutes later, we heard a commotion from upstairs.

I wisped out of the Ghoul's eyelid and floated up the staircase, followed by Wither, and Charlie Vapor passed up through the ceiling.

The bearded still-alive was dashing from room to room, throwing clothes, toiletries, and other oddments into a huge leather suitcase.

"He's off on holler-day," said Charlie.

"No," I said. "Our plan has worked. The still-alives are moving out."

"I hope they take the garlic with them," said Wither.

"There's an open window in one of the front bedrooms," I said. "Let's wisp out and watch."

The other ghosties were already outside, floating above the heads of the high-heeled still-alive, who had popped inside to fetch her shoes, and the two half-sized still-alives and several others who lived on the street.

Nothing happened for a minute or two. Then, the front door flew open, and out tumbled the suitcase, followed by the still-alive with the beard and the ghastly Ghoul, who blew a raspberry and floated back into the house.

16

Leggy Spider

"That's that then," I said, floating joyfully. "The house is ours."

"I wonder where the still-alives will live," said Agatha. "Perhaps they have relatives. An old lady in a felt hat, or a man who invents things."

We floated down to the front door, which swung open on rusty hinges.

"Nothing can go wrong now," said Wither. But we'd only floated as far as the hall door when the Ghoul made such a mean-spirited face that we all floated backward.

"Not like us to float backward like that," said Agatha.

"I didn't know we could," I said.

"Perhaps," said Charlie, "the Ghoul made us jump."

We all floated forward again, but the Ghoul bared his teeth, and once again we all floated back, further this time, to the front door.

"This doesn't feel right," said Gertrude.

"I have goose pimples," said Wither.

"And I," said Agatha, "have a wibbly feeling in my tummy."

"I know that feeling," said Pamela Fraidy. "I get it all the time. It's fear."

Wither folded his bony arms. "You don't mean we're afraid of the Ghoul?"

"Impossible," I said, but a moment later the Ghoul let out a horrific scream, and all seven of us wisped out the front door and up into the sky, and we didn't stop wisping until we reached the chimney pot.

Wither frowned. "Pamela is right. We're afraid of the Ghoul."

"Perhaps," I said, "this is how the still-alives feel when they see us ghosties."

"That would explain their odd behavior," said Charlie.

"There's no excuse for meanness," said Wither.

"But don't you see? The still-alives aren't being mean," I told him. "They run away because they're afraid."

Wither gulped. I think he was swallowing a blub. "So, what now, Tabitha?"

"We make friends with the Ghoul. Yes, we wisp down the chimney, say hello, and wisp back up. This will put the Ghoul in a good mood, and he will want to be our friend."

"And then he won't be mean to us?" asked Wither hopefully.

I nodded. "And then he won't be mean to us.

Who will go first?"

We looked at each other in spooky silence. A plane flew overhead. In the distance, a church bell chimed a spooky chime.

Charlie adjusted his cuff links, his tie, his hat. "I will go first, Tabitha. After all, it is the polite thing to do." And off he wisped down the chimney.

I was about to say how brave he was, how noble and bold, and how he was setting an example for us all, when he wisped back up.

Agatha laughed. "I have to say, Charlie, that was the fastest greeting in history."

"I doubt he got as far as the fireplace," said Wither.

"Do it again, Charlie. This time, I will watch through the window." I wisped over the edge of the roof and floated down to the lounge window.

A moment later, Charlie floated out of the fireplace, his hat pulled down over his eyes, and

he mouthed a hello to the Ghoul's back. By the time the Ghoul had turned around, Charlie had wisped back up to the roof.

Humphrey Bump didn't do much better. A quick wave, and he was back up the chimney, no doubt bumping the brickwork all the way.

The girls were next, Agatha Draft, who blew the Ghoul a kiss, and Gertrude Goo, followed by Wither, who hid his eyes in his top lip. "Oh, please, please, don't be mean to me," he blubbed.

When Pamela's turn came, she floated down the front of the house to join me at the window.

"Hello, Tabitha," she said cheerfully.

"Hello," I said.

Pamela floated up and down for a bit, the breeze blowing her creepy curls, then said, "I thought I'd float down and say hello."

"Hello," I said.

Pamela looked up at the sky, at the wispy,

ghostly clouds. "It's a lovely day, isn't it."

"Yes," I said. "It's lovely."

We floated about for a minute or so, and then I looked Pamela in the eye and asked her if she was afraid.

"I'm not afraid, Tabitha. I'm petrified. I simply cannot say hello to that Ghoul."

The other ghosties were peering down at us from the roof.

"You share my turn with me," I said kindly. Pamela smiled, somewhat bravely, I thought.

"All girls together!"

We held hands and floated in through the lounge window. When I turned round, there was no sign of Pamela. Then I heard a voice from behind the curtain.

"I can say hello better from behind here, Tabitha dear. I can wave too. Though the Ghoul won't see, of course."

The other ghosties—Wither, Charlie and

Humphrey, Gertrude and Agatha—had floated down to the window to watch.

"I guess it's up to me then," I said to myself, then floated into the room.

The Ghoul was floating by the bookcase.

"Hello, Ghoul," I said nervously. "Do you remember me? I'm Tabitha. I hired you to frighten the still-alives, but you scared us ghosties too, by mistake."

I waited. The Ghoul did not respond.

"Ghoul, listen. This has gone quite far enough. We own this house. At least, we do live here. It's our home. And we want you to leave. Immediately."

The Ghoul said nothing.

A moment later, the house began to shake. The books on the bookcase, the bookcase itself, the coffee cups on the coffee table, the vase of flowers, the pictures in their frames, the windows and doors, even the walls shook. They shook and they shook and they shook, and the foundations shuddered and juddered, until the bookcase fell with a terrific thud, the pictures flew from the walls, and the glass coffee table shattered.

From behind the curtain, Pamela let out a frightened sob.

The Ghoul looked frightened too.

"I can do this," I said, "because I'm a poltergeist. And if I can do this to the house, just think what I can do to you."

And for a moment, I thought I had won. But the Ghoul just laughed.

Pamela Fraidy floated out from behind the curtain. "Is he in a good mood now, Tabitha?"

"I'm not sure. Pamela, I think we'd better—"

"Tabitha, you're right. Let's wisp out."

The Ghoul had grown. His eyeballs were like watermelons, his teeth like chainsaws. His shoulders were now so wide they filled the room. He opened his mouth and let out the loudest,

most terrifying scream you could ever imagine. The sheer force sent Pamela and me sailing out of the window, and we found ourselves floating upside down on the front lawn.

"I thought you floated in there to make friends." said Wither. "But you were mean to the Ghoul, and the Ghoul was mean to you."

"You can talk, Wither," said Charlie Vapor. "You can't open your mouth without telling us off for being mean. And what could be more mean than that?"

"Ooh, don't be, um—"

"See?" Charlie said. "Wither, you're the meanest ghosty of all."

Poor Wither did not know which way to wisp.

"You, Charlie, are mean," he blubbed, "and you're mean too, Humphrey, and you three girl-ghosties are mean, and you're all frightfully mean and horrid, so boo snubs and utterly squash." And he floated off into the house.

"Oh dear," said Gertrude.

"You were rather mean to him, Charlie," said Agatha.

Charlie adjusted his cuff links, gazed down at the lawn.

"I'm worried about him now," I said. "In fact, I'm very worried, very worried indeed."

"He'll be all right," said Agatha. "He'll mope for a bit and forget all about it."

"That's not what I meant. Wither is in the house. With the Ghoul."

"I'll float in and look for him," said Charlie. "It was my fault. And I'm the only ghosty who can pass through."

"We'll all look for him," I said. "No need to float inside, Charlie. We can peer in through the windows."

And off we wisped.

We checked the back of the house first, the kitchen, the study, and the back bedroom, and

Gertrude wisped about by the shed. Charlie passed through into the bathroom, then passed back out, wearing the shower cap over the top of his trilby. But no Wither. We floated back over the roof and checked the front bedrooms and the lounge. And still there was no sign of Wither.

A minute later, the front door flew open, and out came the Ghoul, floating off down the street as fast as he could, and I have to say he looked absolutely petrified.

We wondered what was chasing him at first. It was Agatha who spotted it. "Look!" she cried, as the Ghoul vaporized into the afternoon. "The leggy spider."

And there it was. The spider that had so unnerved us all. Not even Pamela was afraid of it now, and Pamela was, and still is, a nervous wreck.

"After meeting that big ugly Ghoul," she told

me, "I don't think I'll ever be afraid of spiders again."

Charlie threw his hat into the air and cheered with delight, and we all floated about on the lawn, laughing our spooky socks off.

"A colossal brute like him," said Agatha, "chased out of the house by a leggy spider!" It was then that Wither floated out of the house.

"Wither," I said, "where have you been?"

"The larder, writing an apologetic poem."

"Weren't you afraid of the Ghoul?"

"I felt too ashamed to be afraid, Tabitha. What are you all laughing at? And what happened to the Ghoul?"

"You were in such a bad mood," said Charlie, "you frightened him off."

Wither made a face. "The Ghoul was afraid of me?"

Agatha and I exchanged looks. Agatha shrugged.

"That's right," I said. "That's what happened."

"You're our hero," said Charlie. He shook Wither by the hand, and we all agreed that this was the polite thing to do.

About the Author and Illustrator

Daren King studied in Bath and lives in London. *Mouse Noses on Toast,* his first book for children, won the Gold Nestlé Children's Prize. *Peter the Penguin Pioneer* was shortlisted for the Blue Peter Award. He is the author of four adult books. *Boxy an Star* was shortlisted for the Guardian First Book Award and longlisted for the Booker Prize.

David Roberts is the award-winning illustrator of over thirty titles. He has had a variety of interesting jobs, such as hair washer, shelf stacker, and hat designer. He was born in Liverpool and now lives in London.